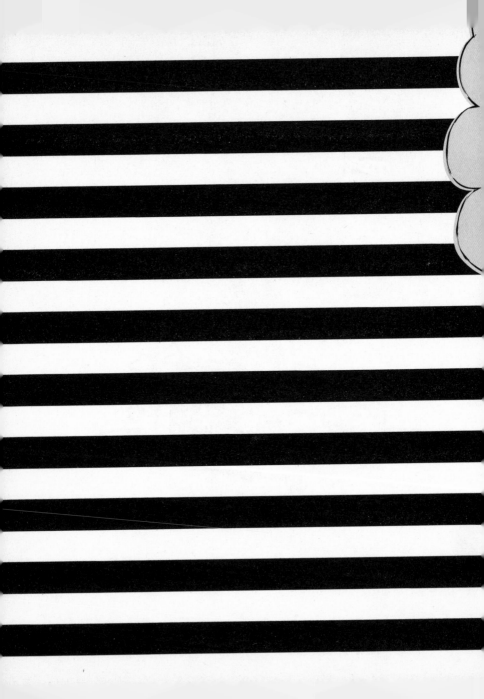

HEiDi HECKELBECK
Goes to Camp!

By Wanda Coven
Illustrated by Priscilla Burris

LITTLE SIMON
New York London Toronto Sydney New Delhi

LITTLE SIMON
An imprint of Simon & Schuster Children's Publishing Division
1230 Avenue of the Americas, New York, New York 10020
Copyright © 2013 by Simon & Schuster, Inc.
All rights reserved, including the right of reproduction in whole or in part in any form.
LITTLE SIMON is a registered trademark of Simon & Schuster, Inc., and associated colophon is a trademark of Simon & Schuster, Inc.
For information about special discounts for bulk purchases, please contact Simon & Schuster Special Sales at 1-866-506-1949 or business@simonandschuster.com.
The Simon & Schuster Speakers Bureau can bring authors to your live event. For more information or to book an event contact the Simon & Schuster Speakers Bureau at 1-866-248-3049 or visit our website at www.simonspeakers.com.
Manufactured in the United States of America 0413 FFG
First Edition 10 9 8 7 6 5 4 3 2 1
Library of Congress Cataloging-in-Publication Data
Coven, Wanda.
Heidi Heckelbeck goes to camp! / by Wanda Coven ; illustrated by Priscilla Burris. — 1st ed.
p. cm. — (Heidi Heckelbeck ; 8)
Summary: Heidi is excited about spending two weeks with Lucy at Camp Dakota, but Lucy's friends from last year ignore Heidi and make her feel unwelcome, leading Heidi to cast a friendship spell on them.
ISBN 978-1-4424-6480-3 (pbk. : alk. paper) — ISBN 978-1-4424-6481-0 (hardcover : alk. paper) — ISBN 978-1-4424-6482-7 (ebook : alk. paper)
[1. Camps—Fiction. 2. Best friends—Fiction. 3. Friendship—Fiction. 4. Witches—Fiction. 5. Magic—Fiction.] I. Burris, Priscilla, ill. II. Title.
PZ7.C83393Hdm 2013
[Fic]—dc23
2012015272

CONTENTS

Chapter 1

A TRUNK FULL OF SPELLS

"Oogie da boinga!" Heidi Heckelbeck said as she grabbed a chocolate chip cookie from the dessert plate.

"What's that supposed to mean?" asked Henry.

"Lucy told me about it," Heidi said. "It means 'wahoo!' at Camp Dakota."

"It also means you have camp spirit," said Dad.

"Well, I have oogie da boinga too," said Henry. "So why can't I go to sleepaway camp?"

"Because you're a SHRIMP," Heidi said.

"Am not."

"Are too."

"Soon Henry will be old enough for sleepaway camp too," Mom said.

"It's going to feel like FOREVER until I'm old enough," said Henry.

"Trust me," Dad said. "It'll go fast."

"And so will this evening if we don't hop to it," said Mom.

"You two go and pack," said Dad. "Henry and I will do the dishes."

Heidi and her best friend, Lucy Lancaster, were leaving for Camp Dakota in the morning. Lucy had gone to Camp Dakota last summer. Now Heidi and Lucy would get to go together for two whole weeks!

Heidi's clothes lay in piles on her bed. Mom had ironed name tags on to all of Heidi's belongings.

"Let's check off the last few things," Mom said.

"Okay," said Heidi.

- ✓ Sneakers
- ✓ Flip-flops
- ✓ Binoculars
- ✓ Baseball cap
- ✓ Socks
- ✓ Stationery
- ✓ Goggles
- ✓ Raincoat
- ✓ Swimsuits
- ✓ Towels
- ✓ Pillow
- ✓ Bathroom kit
- Tap shoes
- Laundry bag

"Now all I need are my tap shoes and a laundry bag."

Heidi grabbed the shoe box from the shelf in her closet. She had tried tap in the school talent show, but that didn't count because she had used a tap-dancing spell. Now she wanted to learn for real.

Mom took one last look at the packing list. "I'll get you a laundry bag from the linen closet," she said.

As soon as Mom left the room, Heidi thought of something else she wanted to pack—something super-important. She kneeled on the carpet

and pulled her keepsake box out from under the bed. She opened the box and took out two things: her *Book of Spells* and her Witches of Westwick medallion. *Mom would never allow me to take these,* thought Heidi. *But what if there's an emergency?*

Heidi looked up and listened for her mom. Then she lifted a stack of clothes and carefully tucked her *Book of Spells* and medallion at the bottom of the trunk. She patted down her clothes as Mom walked back into the room.

"That's it," said Mom, tossing a laundry bag to Heidi. "You're all packed for camp."

"Oogie da boinga!" said Heidi.

Then she shut and latched her trunk.

Chapter 2

WHO'S SHE?

Heidi met Lucy at the Brewster Elementary parking lot. The bus for Camp Dakota had arrived. Some kids had already boarded.

"Time to go!" Heidi said.

She hugged her mom and dad good-bye.

Heidi turned to Henry. "You know what's weird?" she said. "I'm going to miss you."

"I'll miss you too," Henry said. "Write me, okay?"

"Promise," said Heidi. She high-fived her little brother.

Heidi slung her backpack over her shoulder and boarded the bus with Lucy. The girls waved as the bus pulled out. Then they looked at each other and squealed.

"This is going to be the BEST two weeks EVER!" Heidi said.

"I know," said Lucy. "And I can't

wait for you to meet my two camp friends, Jill and Bree."

"Me too," Heidi said.

During the ride the girls played hangman and drew pictures of ladybugs and unicorns. Soon the bus

pulled onto a dirt road lined with pine trees. Lucy pointed to the cabins and the lake at the end of the road. A bunch of campers greeted the bus in the parking lot.

"There they are!" shouted Lucy, waving at her friends from the bus window. She pointed them out to Heidi.

Heidi peeked at the girls. Jill had shoulder-length brown hair, brown eyes, and freckles. Bree had short blond hair and blue eyes. Both girls bounced up and down and waved. *Wow, they sure are happy to see Lucy,* she thought.

Heidi turned to say something to Lucy, but Lucy was already getting off the bus.

"Hey, wait for me!" shouted Heidi, bumping the seats with her backpack as she ran down the aisle.

But no one was listening to Heidi.

Jill, Bree, and Lucy clasped arms and danced in a circle. Then they took turns doing a secret handshake. Heidi tried to follow their moves. It started with a regular handshake, followed by a thumb clasp, a palm slide, and latched fingertips. They topped it off with fist taps, then peace signs across

their eyes. This made Heidi feel a bit left out. Luckily, Lucy noticed.

"This is my friend Heidi," said Lucy.

Jill and Bree stopped talking and looked Heidi up and down.

"Oh, hi," they both said. Then they each grabbed Lucy by an arm.

"Come on, Lucy," said Jill. "Want to see our cabin?" They took off skipping down the path.

Heidi walked behind the girls and listened to them talk. They went on and on about all the fun things they had done last summer.

Some camp greeters followed with Lucy's and Heidi's trunks.

"Remember that huge rainstorm and the big mudslide we made on Huckleberry Hill?" asked Bree.

"That was SO fun," Lucy said.

"I didn't even notice when I scraped my arm!" said Jill.

"I didn't think we'd ever get all that

mud off! It was really caked on!" said Bree.

"What about the time we snuck cookies from the dining room?" asked Lucy.

"We almost got caught," Jill said.

"That was the best part!" said Lucy.

"How about the HAUNTED COMB that flew across the cabin in the middle of the night?" Bree said.

"You threw it and you know it!" said Lucy.

"Did not!" said Bree. "That comb really WAS haunted. Last year was the best!"

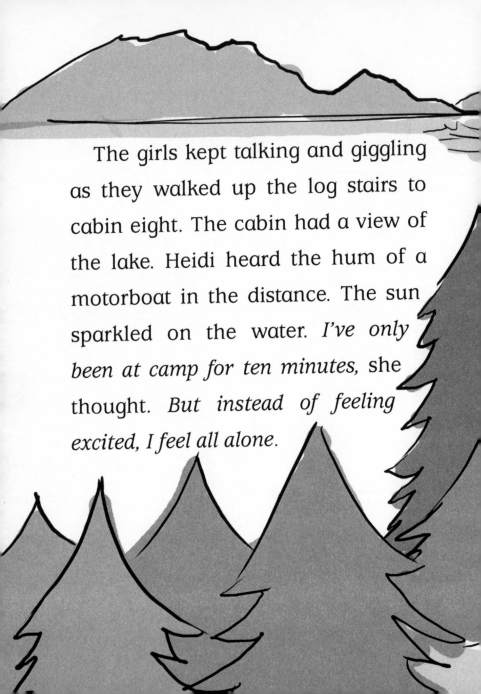

The girls kept talking and giggling as they walked up the log stairs to cabin eight. The cabin had a view of the lake. Heidi heard the hum of a motorboat in the distance. The sun sparkled on the water. *I've only been at camp for ten minutes,* she thought. *But instead of feeling excited, I feel all alone.*

Chapter 3

CLOSETS AND QUILTS

"Lucy, this bed is yours," Bree said as she pointed to a blue-and-white-striped mattress on a metal cot.

Lucy's bed was in between Jill's and Bree's.

Lucy plopped her backpack on the bed. "Where's Heidi going to sleep?"

"Over there, I guess," said Jill as she pointed to a bed on the other side of the cabin. The only other bed on that side was the counselor's.

"Is that okay with you, Heidi?" Lucy asked.

Heidi looked at the lonely bed in

the corner. *No!* she thought. *It's not okay! Why can't Lucy sleep on MY side of the cabin and Jill and Bree sleep on the OTHER side? That would be fair.* But Heidi didn't dare complain. She didn't want Lucy's friends to think she was a baby.

"Sure, it's fine," said Heidi.

She walked over and sat on her mattress. She looked around the cabin. Everyone had a bed and an orange crate. Jill and Bree had already

filled their crates with their bathroom kits, flashlights, bug spray, batteries, and stationery. The back of the cabin had five changing closets. Each one had a cotton curtain with a different print.

There were checks, stripes, flowers, and polka dots. One curtain was plain.

The camp greeters set Lucy's and Heidi's trunks beside their beds and left.

"Let's make your bed, Lucy!" said Bree.

Jill and Bree had already made their beds. Jill's had a swirly polka-dot quilt, and Bree's had a pink-and-orange daisy quilt.

"What does your quilt look like, Lucy?" asked Bree.

"Mine has butterflies," Lucy said as she pulled her quilt from her trunk.

"It's SO cute!" said Jill.

"How about you, Heidi?" asked Lucy. "What's your quilt like?"

"Mine's boring purple with a whole bunch of nothing," said Heidi.

"Oh, I LOVE purple!" Lucy said, trying to make it sound wonderful.

Jill and Bree didn't say anything.

Then the girls picked out closets.

"The
one with
the pink-checked
curtain is yours,"
Bree said.

"Okay," said Lucy. "Heidi,
you can have the one on the other
side of mine."

Heidi looked at her closet. It had a
plain blue curtain that was lopsided.
One of the thumbtacks had fallen out.

Heidi hung up her stuff. Then a
loud bell rang.

"Lunchtime!" said Jill.

Heidi followed the girls out the door. She didn't feel hungry, but she did feel something. It was the same feeling she'd had when she was the new girl at school. She felt like an alien.

Chapter 4

RAH, RAH

Voices chattered and silverware rattled in the log-cabin dining hall. The girls stopped next to the door to look at their table assignments.

"We're at table four," Lucy said, pointing to a list of names.

The girls piled into the dining hall,

but the door snapped shut in Heidi's face. Lucy turned back and opened the door.

"Come on, Heidi," she said.

Heidi followed the girls to table four. Lucy sat next to Jill and Bree. Heidi found an empty seat next to the counselor at the head of the table.

Everyone chatted except Heidi. She just stared at the bowls of food on the table: taco shells, ground beef, corn bread, lettuce, and tomatoes. She helped herself to a glass of red punch.

Even aliens get thirsty, she thought.

Then the counselor tapped her glass with a butter knife. All the girls at the table stopped talking.

"As most of you know, I'm Lila, cabin eight's counselor," she said. "Welcome to Camp Dakota!"

Lila had long, straight brown hair and friendly blue eyes. She looked like an athlete, and she had a golden sun tan.

Lila look around the table and then turned to Heidi. "You must be Heidi."

Heidi nodded.

"I'm glad to have you in my cabin. Tell me, is there anything special you'd like to do at camp?"

"I'd like to tap-dance," said Heidi.

"I like tap too," said Lila. "Did you know I'm the dance teacher?"

Heidi shook her head.

"Well, I am," Lila said. "We're going to have a blast."

Heidi smiled. *Lila's nice,* she thought. *Maybe camp won't be so bad after all.* She ate half a taco and had some more punch.

At the end of lunch, Lila walked to the front of the dining hall. Two other counselors ran to join her—one had red hair in a ponytail and the other had short black hair.

"Welcome to Camp Dakota!" the red-haired girl said. "I'm Jenna."

"I'm Paige," said the black-haired girl.

"I'm Lila."

"First, we have to go over camp rules," said Paige. "So listen up! Rule number one: Always have a buddy at the beach."

Lila held up a big sign that said BUDDY UP!

"Rule number two: Always stay on the camp's grounds," Jenna said.

Paige held up a sign that had a map of the camp. It said STAY PUT!

"Rule number three: Always follow the counselors' instructions," said Lila.

Jenna held up a sign that said WHO'S THE BOSS? Then she flipped it over, and it said WE ARE!

"Now for the camp no-no's," said Jenna.

"No matches."

"No hair-dryers."

"No hand-held devices."

"No water balloons or shaving cream!"

"Unless we say so!" added Lila.

"No radios," continued Jenna.

"No food in the cabins."

"No rubber duckies!"

"And no rubber chickens!"

The campers laughed.

"Okay, we're only joking about the rubber duckies and chickens," Paige

said. "But we're not kidding when we say 'No monkey business.' Follow the rules and be safe."

"Okay, sign-up sheets for activities are at the back of the room!" said Lila. "If you have any questions, come see us."

Everyone began to talk and clear dishes. Heidi scraped the food from her plate into the trash and put her dishes into a plastic tub. Then she headed for the sign-up tables. Jill and Bree were still stuck to Lucy like Super

Glue. Heidi stood behind them.

"What are you going to sign up for?" asked Lucy.

"Tap-dance, riding, arts and crafts, swimming, and basketball," Heidi said excitedly.

"Me too!" squealed Lucy. "Except

instead of tap, I'm going to take gymnastics with Jill and Bree."

"Sounds good," said Heidi. *Except for the part about Jill and Bree,* she thought.

"So, what do you think of camp so far?" asked Lucy. "Isn't it fun?"

"It's a blast," Heidi said. "Rah, rah."

Chapter 5

KER-FLUNK!

Heidi stuffed her tap shoes in her backpack.

"See you at riding!" Lucy said as she left for gymnastics.

Jill and Bree followed Lucy down the cabin stairs. They didn't say good-bye to Heidi.

I wonder why those two don't like me, Heidi wondered. She slung her backpack over her shoulder and headed for tap class.

Lila taught the class how to shuffle.

"I want you to brush the floor with the ball of your foot forward and backward," she said. "Like this."

Lila brushed her foot across the

floor from front to back. "Try it with me," said Lila.

Heidi did a shuffle. She liked it when her tap shoes clacked on the floor. Then Lila taught the class to shim sham.

"A shim sham is a shuffle and a step," said Lila as she turned on some music.

The class did a combination of steps: Shim sham. Jump. Toe. Step. They did it again and again to the music. *This is so much fun!* thought Heidi. *I can't wait to show Lucy.* Then Heidi's heart sank. She remembered that Lucy had been taken over by Jill and Bree. *Maybe they'll be nicer to me at riding,* she thought.

Heidi arrived at the riding ring in a sweatshirt, jeans, and scuffed cowboy boots. She'd had to borrow a stinky helmet from the stable. Lucy, Jill, and

Bree had on riding pants, hunting coats, and fancy riding helmets. Bree stared at Heidi's outfit.

"Are you really going to ride in THAT?" asked Bree.

Heidi looked down at her outfit.

"We all wore jeans when we rode last year," Lucy said. "Remember?"

"Let's just go and choose our horses," said Jill.

The girls ran to the stables. Each stall had a name above the door. Lucy chose a horse named Peaches. Jill chose Tinkerbell, and Bree chose Sundance. Heidi got a horse named Fred.

"He's gentle," said Jenna. "And he always follows the other horses."

Jenna helped Heidi get into her saddle. But Fred did not follow the other horses. He stood still, eating grass. Jenna tried to get Fred to move. But Fred wouldn't budge.

Heidi sighed. *Not even a dumb horse likes me,* she thought.

Later, in swim class, everyone had to pick a buddy.

"Want to be buddies?" asked Lucy.

"Sure," Heidi said.

First the girls had to take a swim test. Heidi had never gone swimming in a lake before. The lake water looked dark and murky. *What if there are snapping turtles in there?* Heidi

thought. She tightly shut her eyes and jumped in the water.

Heidi then swam a few strokes, but all she could think about were snapping turtles. She was so scared that she grabbed the safety pole before the test was over. That meant Heidi had flunked the test. Now she would be placed in Beginners.

In the meantime, Lucy, Bree, and Jill had passed

the test with flying colors, so they were placed in Intermediates.

All day everything seemed to go wrong. On the basketball court nobody passed the ball to Heidi. In

arts and crafts, they ran out of beads, so Heidi had to braid the strings of her friendship bracelets instead. At Campfire, Heidi got squished between two strange girls. And to top it off, the smoke blew right into her face.

I'm getting out of here, thought Heidi.

She wiggled off the log and ran back to the cabin.

Nobody noticed
Heidi had gone.

Chapter 6

SUGAR AND SPICE

Heidi sat on her bed and pulled out a sheet of turtle stationery. She wrote:

Dear Henry,

Camp stinks. The beds are really squeaky. The bathrooms are smelly. And the lake is full of snapping

71

turtles. The only friends I have are mosquitoes.

Yours truly,

Heidi

PS Stay out of my room—or else!

Heidi stuck the letter in an envelope and sighed. *Jill and Bree have taken my best friend prisoner,* she thought. *If only they liked me, then camp would be fun.* Suddenly, Heidi had a wild idea. *What if I MAKE them like me?*

Heidi flung open her trunk and pulled out her *Book of Spells*. She flipped through the pages and found a spell called A Friendly Foe. *Perfect,* she thought. *A friendly foe is an enemy who becomes a friend.* She read over the spell.

A Friendly Foe

Do people dislike you for no reason? Are you the kind of witch who always feels left out? Would you like to make friends with your enemies? Then this is the spell for you!

Ingredients:
1 cup of fruit punch
1 stick of powdered candy
1 teaspoon of cinnamon sugar
1 friendship bracelet for each foe
1 empty water bottle

Shake all the ingredients together in the water bottle. Hold your Witches of Westwick medallion in your left hand. Close your eyes and place your right hand over the bottle.

Chant the following words:

Oh, SWEET MAGICAL BREW
FILLED WITH SUGAR, AND SPICE,
MAKE [NAME OF PERSON(S)]
GO FROM MEAN TO NICE!

Remove the bracelets.
When the bracelets are dry,
the spell has been cast.

Note: If the bracelet has contact with water, the spell will wear off.

Heidi skipped over the note in small letters at the bottom of the spell and read back over the list of ingredients. Then she grabbed an empty sports water bottle from her orange crate. *I can get the fruit punch and cinnamon sugar from the dining hall,* she thought. *The camp store sells powdered candy. And I can use the friendship bracelets I made in arts and crafts. So simple!*

Heidi memorized the spell. Then she hid her *Book of Spells* at the bottom of her trunk. She heard campers talking as they walked back to their cabins. *Campfire must be over,* she thought. She quickly put on her panda pajamas and slipped into bed.

Tomorrow is going to be a better day. . . .

SHA-ZING!

The next day Jill, Bree, and Lucy left for breakfast without Heidi.

"Hurry up!" called Lucy from the stairs.

"Be right there," Heidi called back.

Heidi dumped her earplugs onto the bed. *I'll hide the cinnamon sugar*

81

in my earplug case, she thought.
She shoved the empty case into her
pocket, grabbed the water bottle, and
ran to the dining hall.

At breakfast Heidi
slipped a teaspoon
into her pocket.
Then she filled
her water bottle
with one cup of
fruit punch. Bree
gave her a funny look. Heidi smiled
and excused herself from the table.
She found the cinnamon sugar at
the toaster station. She poured some

sugar into her earplug case and snapped the lid shut.

"What are you up to?" asked Lucy.

Heidi jumped. "Oh, nothing."

"Hmm," said Lucy. "Well, we should get going. The first activity is about to start."

The girls left the dining hall and headed toward their activities.

Heidi had some free time after tap. She raced to the camp store and bought two striped straws filled with powdered candy. *I'll use cherry for the spell,* she thought. *And I'll keep the grape one for me.* Then she zoomed back to the empty cabin. Heidi had to

hurry. The girls would be back soon to change before riding.

Heidi tore the top off the cherry straw and dumped the red powder into the fruit punch. Then she added a teaspoon of cinnamon sugar. Heidi shook the water bottle. Then she opened it back up and dropped two friendship bracelets inside. She held

her medallion in one
of her hands. Then
she shut her eyes,
placed her other
hand over the
bottle, and
chanted
the spell.
The mixture
bubbled for a few moments. Then it
became still.

Heidi took the friendship bracelets
out of the bottle with her finger. In a
few moments they were dry . . . and
magical!

When Jill and Bree returned to change, Heidi handed the bewitched bracelets to them.

"Uh, thanks?" Bree said, not really sure what to say.

Heidi gave a regular bracelet to Lucy.

The girls slipped on their bracelets.

Sha-zing!

The magic began to work.

"Wow," said Bree. "This is the most beautiful friendship bracelet I've ever seen!"

"Same with mine," Jill said. Jill and Bree each hooked an elbow with

Heidi and walked with her to the stables. Lucy hurried after them.

At the stables Jill gave the best horse to Heidi. "I want you to ride Tinkerbell today," she said. "She's the nicest horse of all."

"Thanks!" said Heidi.

All afternoon Jill and Bree did everything to please Heidi.

"Sit with me!" begged Jill.

"Be my partner!" pleaded Bree.

"You are the BEST artist, Heidi!"

"Please show us your tap steps!"

"Be my best friend!"

"No, be MINE!"

On the dock at swimming, Lucy pulled Heidi aside. "What on earth is going on?" she asked.

"Beats me," Heidi said, trying not to smile. "But it's a nice change—don't you think?"

"It's a little weird, if you ask me," said Lucy.

Then Heidi, Jill, and Bree held hands and jumped off the float.

Splash!

But when they popped up for air, something had changed.

"What are YOU doing here?" asked Bree.

"Aren't you in Beginners?" added Jill.

Oh no! Heidi thought. *The spell has worn off!* She swam to the ladder. Then

Heidi wrapped herself in a towel, slipped on her flip-flops, and hurried to the cabin. *If only they had liked me for real,* she thought. *But it was just the dumb spell.* Heidi kicked a pinecone on the path.

NOW what am I going to do?

Chapter 8

CHICKEN TALK

"You're back early," Lila said as Heidi walked into the cabin.

Heidi tried to say something, but she couldn't. Her eyes filled with tears.

"Come sit," said Lila. She spread a towel across her bed and offered Heidi a big box of pink tissues.

Heidi sat down and pulled out a tissue.

"What's up?" asked Lila.

"It's Jill and Bree," Heidi said in between sniffles. "They're mean to me, and they hog all of Lucy's time."

"Have you talked to them about it?" asked Lila.

"No," said Heidi.

"Well, you should," said Lila. "You need to find out what's going on."

"I'm too chicken," said Heidi. "What if they really hate me?"

Lila patted Heidi on the back. "They have no reason to hate you," she said. "They're probably just jealous."

"JEALOUS?" questioned Heidi. "Of ME?"

"Yes, of *you*," said Lila. "You're a total package!"

Heidi wiped her nose with a tissue.

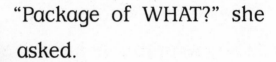

"Package of WHAT?" she asked.

Lila smiled at Heidi. "Package of F-U-N," she said, messing up Heidi's wet hair.

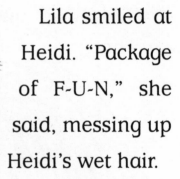

Heidi let out a small laugh.

"Listen, I have to get ready for my next class," said Lila, getting up. "Tell me how it goes."

"*B-r-r-r-ock, b-r-r-r-ock,*" squawked Heidi.

"You can't chicken out," said Lila. "Be brave!"

Lila gave Heidi a hug. "Your bathing suit got me all wet," she said.

"That's because I'm a wet chicken," said Heidi.

"You need to be a *brave* chicken," said Lila. Then she hurried down the steps.

Heidi got dressed in her changing closet. Then she flopped onto her bed and waited for the girls to come back from swimming. *What am I going to say?* she thought. *Hey, guys. Why do you hate me so much?*

Chapter 9

OOGIE DA BOINGA!

The cabin door banged open. Heidi jumped to her feet.

"What's up, Heidi?" asked Lucy. "Everything okay?"

"Not really," said Heidi.

"What's wrong?" asked Lucy.

Heidi looked at Jill and Bree. She

pushed the chicken thoughts out of
her head. "How come you guys are
so mean to me?" she asked. "I really
don't like to be treated that way."

Jill and Bree looked surprised, but
neither one said a word.

"Heidi's right, you know," said Lucy. "You haven't been nice to her at all. How come?"

Jill and Bree looked at each other. Then Jill put up her hands. "Okay, okay," she said. "I guess we were afraid that Heidi had taken our place. We didn't want to lose Lucy as our friend."

"Are you kidding?" asked Lucy. "You're not going to lose me as a friend. I'll always be friends with you!" Then she turned to Heidi. "And I'll always be friends with Heidi, too."

Lucy smiled at Heidi.

"Why can't we *all* be friends?"

asked Heidi. "I'm really not an evil,
friend-stealing monster, you know."

"Now THAT would be an ugly
monster," Bree said, cracking a smile.

The girls all laughed.

"I guess we HAVE been kind of
rotten," admitted Jill.

"I'm sorry that we made you feel bad, Heidi," said Bree.

Heidi felt so relieved. "I only wish I had said something sooner," she replied.

"I wish I had too," said Lucy. She put her hand in front of Heidi. "Friends?" she asked.

Heidi put her hand on top of Lucy's. "Friends," she said.

Jill and Bree put their hands on top of the others. "Friends," they said.

"You know what?" Heidi said. "I just
felt it for the first time at camp!"
"What?" asked Lucy.

"Oogie da boinga!" said Heidi.

Lucy's eyes got wide. "I felt it too!" she said. "Oogie da boinga!"

"So did I!" said Jill.

"Me too!" said Bree.

"Oogie da boinga!" they all said together.

Lucy, Jill, and Bree changed out of their wet swimsuits. Then all four girls walked arm in arm to lunch.

Chapter 10

"DAKOTA" MEANS "FRiENDS"

A week later Heidi sat on her bed and wrote another letter to her brother.

Dear Henry,

You know what stinks most about camp? It's almost over. I come home in three days! Lucy and I are going to miss our cabinmates and counselor so much. I love my friends. Did

you know "DaKota" is a Native
American word for "friends"?
Pretty cool.

Last night we had a shaving
cream fight. Everyone got a can
of shaving cream. Then we had
a FOAM WAR. Here's a picture of
us with foam hairdos and foam
beards. Like Lucy's Mohawk?

Big news! I can ride a horse! My horse, Fred, didn't like me at first. He could tell I was a scaredy-cat, but now we're buds. I sneak him carrots and sugar cubes from the dining hall every day.

One of my favorite things about camp is Campfire. The

counselors play
guitars, and we sing
songs and roast
marshmallows. I ate
five s'mores last
night!

Guess what? We won the
neatest cabin award! We got
FREE candy at the camp store.
I picked fireballs, root beer
barrels, and a Tootsie Pop.

Tonight we're going to write our names on the cabin wall. We found names of campers from the 1920s! I wonder what camp was like in those days? Did they have shaving cream fights? Did they even HAVE shaving cream back then?

Tomorrow night is the talent show. I'm doing a tap routine (without spells).

See ya soon, shrimp!

Love,

Heidi

PS I didn't see a single snapping turtle!

PPS I can't wait for BOTH of us to come back next time.

PPPS Oogie da boinga!

Check out the next book starring

HEIDI HECKELBECK

Heidi woke up and opened the blinds. The sun sparkled on the fresh snow. It was well over a foot deep. *There's no way I'll find the charm bracelet today,* she thought.

Heidi and Henry got ready for school and headed for the bus stop. The snowplow had left steep snowbanks on either side of the driveway. Heidi spotted something

An excerpt from *Heidi Heckelbeck and the Christmas Surprise*

in the tire tracks. She stooped down and lifted something from the snow. Heidi gasped. *The charm bracelet!* she thought. Then she took a closer look. Most of the charms had been crushed by the snowplow. *Oh no! NOW what am I going to do?*

Heidi found Lucy the moment she got to school.

"I have TERRIBLE news," said Heidi.

"What's wrong?" Lucy asked.

"I lost my mom's charm bracelet in the snow yesterday," said Heidi. "It must've slipped off."

"You're kidding!" cried Lucy.

"It gets worse," said Heidi. "I found the bracelet in our driveway before school. But it got smashed by the snowplow."

"Oh no!" Lucy cried. "What are you going to do?"

"I'm going to try to fix it after school," said Heidi.

"Not to be mean," said Lucy, "but it would take a magician to fix that bracelet."

"I know," said Heidi. "All I need is a little magic."

An excerpt from *Heidi Heckelbeck and the Christmas Surprise*